# TALES FROM WALES

Published by Dragon Books 1984
Granada Publishing Limited
8 Grafton Street, London W1X 3LA

Copyright © Harri Webb 1984
Illustrations copyright © Lesley Bruce 1984

*British Library Cataloguing in Publication Data*

Webb, Harri
  Tales from Wales.
  I. Title
  823'.914 J          PZ7

  ISBN 0-246-12088-6

Printed and bound in Great Britain by
Collins, Glasgow

# TALES
# FROM
# WALES

*Retold by*
*HARRI WEBB*

*Illustrated by*
*LESLEY BRUCE*

DRAGON BOOKS
Granada Publishing

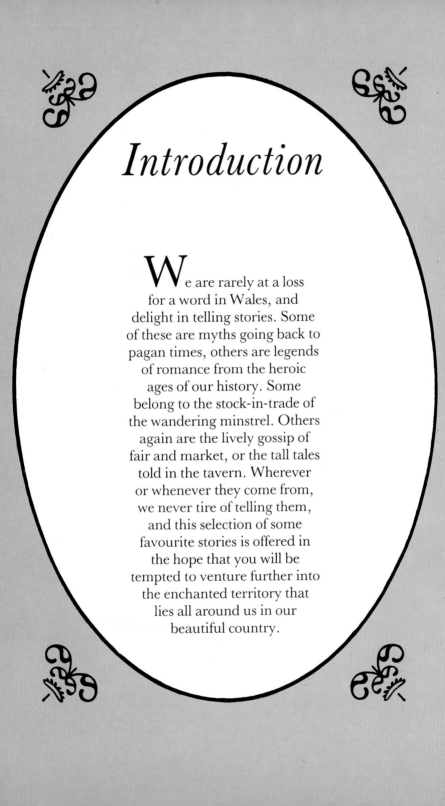

# Introduction

We are rarely at a loss for a word in Wales, and delight in telling stories. Some of these are myths going back to pagan times, others are legends of romance from the heroic ages of our history. Some belong to the stock-in-trade of the wandering minstrel. Others again are the lively gossip of fair and market, or the tall tales told in the tavern. Wherever or whenever they come from, we never tire of telling them, and this selection of some favourite stories is offered in the hope that you will be tempted to venture further into the enchanted territory that lies all around us in our beautiful country.

# Contents

Branwen 7

Pwyll, Prince of Dyfed 13

Pwyll and Rhiannon 17

Pryderi 21

Kilhwch and Olwen 27

The Bride of Flowers 39

The Land Beneath the Waves 46

The Dream of Maxen Wledig 52

Rhonabwy's Dream 57

Saint David 63

Gelert 68

The Lady of the Lake 72

The Curse of Pantannas 78

The Haunting of the Red Castle 83

The Hazel Staff 89

# BRANWEN

In the first ages, Britain was known by its sons and daughters as the Island of the Mighty. Its ruler was Bendigeidfran, called Brân the Blessed, a man of giant stature. And as he was the goodliest of men, so his sister, the Lady Branwen, was accounted the fairest of women. And with great rejoicing she was betrothed to the King of Ireland's son. But at the bridal feast her quarrelsome cousin Efnissien did much harm to the horses of the Irish wedding guests. Brân decided to make good the damage by adding to the bride's rich dowry his most precious possession. This was *Pair Dadeni*, the Cauldron of Rebirth, which had this quality: that any dead warrior who was cast into it would be restored to life as he was at his best, except that he would not regain his speech. He hoped that the feelings of his guests would be soothed by such a valuable gift.

Then the bridal party set sail from Aber Menai in thirteen ships. In her new country the Princess was at first welcomed and well received, but before long the news spread there of the insult done by Efnissien, and Branwen was sent from the court to work among the kitchen wenches. All communication was cut off between the two islands, so that no ship or boat or coracle passed between them. But Branwen secretly reared a starling in a quiet corner of the great kitchen, and taught it to speak, and sent it across the sea as a messenger. It flew to Brân's castle at Caer Seiont in Arfon, which today we call Caernarfon. And so Brân learnt of the wrong done to his sister, and immediately assembled a great host, and so many ships that they resembled a forest on the sea.

It was impossible to conceal preparations on such a vast scale, so that when the invading host reached Ireland, they found that the enemy had retreated to the farther bank of a wide river. Brân, seeing this, declared in a loud voice, *A vo penn bid bont*, 'He who would be a chief, let him be a bridge', and flung his giant frame across the water, and the host passed over him.

There followed such carnage between the two armies that few survived. Of all the hosts of the Island of the Mighty only seven were left alive. Brân himself perished in the onslaught, wounded in the foot by a poisoned spear. And when he knew that his end was near, he commanded his comrades to strike off his head, and take it with them and bury it in Britain under the White Hill that looks across the Narrow Sea, so that in death as in life he should guard the Island of the Mighty.

'And,' he said – for he also had the gift of prophecy – 'you will be a long time on the road. In Harlech you will feast for seven years, and the Birds of Rhiannon will come to you and sing so sweetly that you will not heed the passing of time. And my head will be as pleasant company to you as ever it was upon my body. At Gwalas in Penfro you will be four-score years, and my

8

head will be with you, until you open the door that looks towards Cornwall. Then you may no longer tarry but must set forth straightway and bury my head.'

And it all fell out as Brân had foretold.

Branwen was with the seven when they came to land at Aber Alaw, and there she sat down to rest. And Branwen said, 'Woe is me that ever I was born. Two great islands have been destroyed because of me.' Then she uttered a loud groan and there her heart broke and she died. And they made for her a four-sided grave on the banks of the Alaw.

Then the seven journeyed on to Harlech, and the Birds of Rhiannon, whose home is beneath the waves, flew to them and sang for them, and all the songs they ever heard were mere discord compared with such singing. And the birds seemed to be at a great distance from them over the water, yet they appeared as distinct as if they were close by. And their entertainment continued seven years.

At the end of the seventh year they went forth to Gwalas, an island in the Pembroke sea. There they found a spacious hall. Two of its doors were open, but the third, which looked towards Cornwall, was closed. And there they remained four-score years.

The head of Brân had been with them all this time, as fresh and as lively as if it were still on his shoulders, and he so entertained them that they were unaware of the passage of time.

And so they remained until, one day, Heilyn, the son of Gwynn, opened the door that looked towards

Cornwall. And at once they were conscious of all the evils that had ever beset them, and of all the friends and companions they had lost, and of all the miseries that had befallen them, as if it had happened on that very spot, and especially they were grieved by the loss of their lord. And so they left that place and travelled until they reached the White Hill overlooking the Narrow Sea, and there they buried the head of Brân.

And the Island of the Mighty remained free from invasion from that time onward, until King Arthur in his pride unearthed the head of Brân, declaring that only by the might and fame of King Arthur could the land be defended. And then it was that the prowling Saxons who infested the Narrow Sea scrambled ashore and began to set up their pirate kingdoms in the Isle of Britain.

# PWYLL, PRINCE OF DYFED

Pwyll, Prince of Dyfed, Lord of its Seven Regions, was minded to go hunting, and it pleased him to ride towards Glyn Cuch. In that steep, dark valley he heard the baying of hounds which were not of his pack, and soon he saw them circling for the kill a stag which he himself had hunted. And they were the strangest hounds he had ever

seen, with shining white bodies and glistening red ears. A hunter came towards him on a light grey horse, and they exchanged the wonted courtesies. It turned out they were both princes, but whereas Pwyll's princedom was of this world, that of the other was in Annwn, which is the Other World. His name was Arawn, and he and Pwyll soon became friends.

'There is a king called Havgan,' said Arawn, 'who is always at war with me. If you will go to the Other World in my stead and in my likeness, which I will contrive by enchantment, and rule there for one year, you will be able to rid me of this tyrant. Likewise, in your stead and in your likeness, I will rule over your realm. A year from tonight in a battle at the ford, you will be the victor and you will overthrow Havgan. But you must not deliver the final stroke which will kill him, for whenever I have done this in the past, he has recovered and risen up to contend with me as strongly as ever.'

Arawn led Pwyll to his new kingdom, which he found was the most beautiful place he had ever seen. There Pwyll ruled for one year, living in great comfort in a spacious court, well supplied with meat and drink, and no stinting of minstrelsy or good cheer or the pleasures of the chase.

Then the time came for the encounter at the ford. Havgan was there with all his warriors. A herald stepped forward to proclaim mortal combat between two great chieftains. In the guise of Arawn, Pwyll struck so shrewdly that the enemy's shield was shattered. Then Havgan implored him, 'For the love of Heaven, since thou has begun to slay me, complete thy work.'

14

'I may yet repent of dealing thy death blow,' said Pwyll. 'Slay thee who may, I will not do so.'

'Bear me hence,' said Havgan. 'My death has come.'

And Pwyll took possession of all that belonged to Havgan, and received the homage of his warriors also.

Then Pwyll returned to Glyn Cuch and again met Arawn. They rejoiced to see one another, and each was restored to his proper likeness.

'There is now but one lord in the whole realm of Annwn,' said Pwyll, 'and it is Arawn.'

So the two men took leave of one another, and Pwyll rode back to his own place. He gathered his nobles together and enquired of them how his rule had been during the past year.

'Lord,' they said, 'thy wisdom was never so great, and thou wast never so free in bestowing thy gifts, and thy justice was never more worthily seen than in this year.'

'By Heaven,' he said, 'for all the good you have enjoyed, you should thank him who hath been with you, for thus this matter hath been.'

'Verily, Lord,' they said, 'render thanks unto Heaven that thou hast such a fellowship, and withold not from us the favour which we have enjoyed for this past year.'

'I take Heaven to witness that I will not withold it,' answered Pwyll.

16

# PWYLL AND RHIANNON

The chief place in all of the Seven Regions of Dyfed was at Narberth where there was a mound which had this quality: that whoever should sit there could never leave it unless he had either received wounds or blows or should see a wonder.

'I am not afraid of any of these,' said Pwyll, 'and I should like to see a wonder.' So he went up to the top of the mound. There he saw a lady riding on a white horse

and clad in a garment of shining gold. And although her horse's pace seemed to be gentle, yet no other horse in all his realms could overtake it. After three days, with all the strength of his best horses quite spent, Pwyll himself went out and called to the lady, requesting to know her errand. Gracefully she reined in her horse beside him and told him he himself was the object of her quest. She was the lady Rhiannon, daughter of Hefeydd Hên, and her kinsmen wished her to marry against her will. But her heart was set upon Pwyll, Prince of Dyfed.

'By Heaven,' said Pwyll, 'if I could choose between all the ladies in the world, thee would I choose.'

A twelvemonth hence there was to be a feast at the court of Hafeydd Hên and there Pwyll was to ask for the lady's hand. They took their leave, she to return to her father's court, he to meet his companions at the mound.

Within the year Pwyll and his companions set out on their joyous journey. They were welcomed and feasted, and the lady sat at her father's right hand. During the feast a tall young man came boldly into the hall and craved a boon of Pwyll as the noblest of the company.

'Gladly,' said Pwyll, 'for the sake of the day.' Whereupon Rhiannon cried out, for this was the young man whom her kindred wished her to marry against her will. His name was Gwawl, the son of a wealthy chieftain, and his boon was to be Rhiannon's hand. But the word of a prince is not lightly broken, else he is shamed. And Pwyll had given his word to Gwawl.

18

Then Rhiannon said secretly to Pwyll, 'Bestow me upon him, for I have a plan that ensures that I will never be his. Take thou this small bag, see that thou keep it well. I will engage to become his bride a twelvemonth hence and he will give a feast of his own. Be thou there, with thy hundred comrades concealed in the orchard, and be thyself in rags, and beg for a bagful of food. Show him this bag, for it is a bag that can never be filled.'

At the end of the twelvemonth it all came to pass as the lady had foretold. Pwyll, clad in coarse raiment, came to the feast with his beggar's bag, Gwawl caused it to be filled till all his store was exhausted, then he himself stepped into the bag, saying, 'Enough has been put therein.' Whereupon Pwyll swiftly closed the bag over Gwawl's head, fastened it with a thong, and blew his horn. The hundred that were with Pwyll seized the host that were with Gwawl, and cast them into prison. Then Pwyll threw them the bag, and as they came in every one of Pwyll's knights struck a blow on the bag, and asked, 'What is here?'

'A badger,' was the reply. And this was the first time that the game of The Badger in the Bag was ever played, and a very rough game it is.

Gwawl pleaded for mercy, and Rhiannon decreed that he should no longer be punished, as long as he released her from her betrothal vows, and never sought revenge for his treatment.

When Gwawl had promised all this, Pwyll and Rhiannon took their leave of the court of Hefeydd Hên, and returned together to Narberth.

# PRYDERI

When a son was born to Pwyll and Rhiannon there was great rejoicing, and six women were set to keep watch on him. But they became drowsy and while they slept the boy disappeared. Fearing that they would be punished or even put to death, they decided to kill one of the litter of a staghound bitch, and smear the blood on the hands and face of Rhiannon, and swear that she was responsible for the loss of her son. They invented a frightful story of her violence and of their own struggles to subdue her. And their story was believed.

Pwyll loved Rhiannon, and would not have her put away, but a penance had to be devised by the wise men of Dyfed, and it was this: that she should remain in the palace of Narberth for seven years, beside the mounting-block near the main gate, and should relate her story to all who came by, and that she should offer to the guests and strangers, if they would permit her, to carry them on her back into the palace. But few visitors would offer such discourtesy to a gentle lady.

Now at this time Teyrnon was Lord of Gwent, at the extremity of the land far distant from Dyfed. He was the owner of the best mare in the world, which every

May Eve gave birth to a foal, which immediately
vanished. Teyrnon decided to discover the cause of this,
and had the mare brought into the palace and closely
watched. On the next May Eve the mare gave birth to a
fine colt. Teyrnon heard a great noise as of a storm and
many voices wailing, and a huge arm came through the
window and a great claw seized the young colt. Teyrnon
drew his sword and struck off the arm at the elbow before

it could carry the young beast away. He rushed out but could see nothing because it was so dark. When he returned, beside the colt there was an infant boy in swaddling clothes.

It was the same night that Rhiannon had born Pwyll his first child, but her story was not known in Gwent. The child's clothes were satin, he was strong and well-formed, and Teyrnon and his wife decided to rear

23

him as their own. They had him christened Gwri Gwallt Euryn which means golden haired boy, and in his fourth year he was big enough to be given the colt that had been born on the same night as he had appeared.

Then they heard the story of Rhiannon and how she had been accused of killing her baby son and of her bitter penance. And Teyrnon looked hard at the boy, and it seemed to him that he had never seen so close a likeness between father and son as between this child and

the Prince of Dyfed. For the semblance of Pwyll was well-known to him, for he had been one of Pwyll's followers in days gone by. He took counsel with his wife, and they agreed that Gwri must be Pwyll's son. And they decided to return him to his father so that the grievous lot of Rhiannon should be brought to an end. Forthwith they set out for Dyfed, with Gwri riding the horse that was the one age with himself.

When they reached Narberth Rhiannon was at her penance, but they refused to hear her story or be carried on her back. They went into the palace, where there was a feast prepared for Pwyll, who had returned from a circuit of his territories. Teyrnon took the boy by the hand and set him before Pwyll and told the whole

story of his finding and of his rearing in Gwent. All those present marvelled at the likeness between man and boy and agreed that the child could be none other than the son of Pwyll. And so the lady Rhiannon was clear of any guilt and free of any punishment and her penance was lifted from her and she was fully restored to her honour and high position. The boy his foster-parents had named Golden-Hair now assumed the name his natural mother had given him when he was born, Pryderi, which means Anxiety, for she had forseen her fate. Teyrnon departed for his own country nor would he accept any of the rich gifts offered to him, only the promise of the support of the Prince of Dyfed and of his faithful friendship.

Pryderi was brought up as was fitting the son of a prince and in the fullness of time he succeeded his father as the Lord of the Seven Regions of Dyfed. To these seven he added three others, and the land prospered in his time.

# KILHWCH AND OLWEN

Kilhwch was a fine young man whose mother had died, but not before he had learned from her that it was his destiny to marry but one woman, Olwen, the daughter of Yspaddaden, the Chief Giant. And as soon as he heard the name of Olwen spoken, the youth blushed, and love for the maiden diffused itself through all his frame, though he had never seen her. He was well-born and close cousin to King Arthur himself, so he decided to go to the royal court and discover where the lady could be found. He set off on his dapple grey horse, with his two brindled greyhounds like two sea-swallows sporting around him as he rode. His sword was sharp, his war-horn was of ivory, and sitting high on his noble steed he was a majestic sight. When he came to King Arthur's palace the porter hastened to tell the king that the man at the gate was the goodliest he had ever seen.

Kilhwch was made welcome in the court and explained his mission. Immediately messengers were sent out to discover the whereabouts of the giant's daughter. A whole host searched for a twelvemonth, but in vain. So Kilhwch decided to make his own search, together with a few faithful friends selected by Arthur from among his most staunch companions: Kai and Bedwyr and Gwalchmai, and also Gwrhyr who knew all languages, and Menw who could overcome monsters by casting spells.

After some time they came upon a shepherd, who told them that the flocks he tended were the flocks of

Yspaddaden. The giant, he said, slew all men who came courting his daughter, for his life would end when his daughter was wed. The shepherd was Yspaddaden's own brother, who had suffered great wrong at the giant's hands, and his wife was sister to Kilhwch's own mother. Unknown to the giant, the shepherd and his wife bravely arranged that Olwen should visit them.

As soon as Kilhwch saw her he knew at once that she was the lady he had loved for so long. Her golden hair and white skin, her bright eyes and rosy cheeks put him in mind of the loveliest flowers of the fields and groves, and wherever she walked the white blossoms of the meadow trefoil seemed to spring up where her light footstep touched the ground.

Kilhwch and his companions determined to win her at once. For three days they called upon the giant, and every day Yspaddaden hurled his spears at them. But the champions stood their ground and hurled them back at him, to damaging effect.

Then, to gain time, the giant, fearing for his life, laid down a whole series of impossibly difficult tasks that would have to be accomplished before any suitor could win his daughter's hand.

First they must obtain the sword of Gwrnach the Black Giant, who forbad all men to enter his castle.

Then they must find Mabon, the son of the great huntsman Modron, who had been stolen from his mother when he was only three days old.

Next they must gather nine bushels of flax-seed to grow the flax that would be spun into Olwen's bridal veil.

Then they must obtain the beard of Dillus the robber, to be woven into a leash which alone could tether Aned and Aethlem, the dogs that would be needed for the hunting of the Great Riving Boar.

Then they had to hunt also the Boar of North Britain, Ysgithrwyn, whose tusk alone could shave the beard of the Chief Giant.

Lastly they had to get the blood of the Black Witch, which was also necessary for the shaving of Yspaddaden.

The champions forthwith addressed themselves to these tasks. First, to gain admittance to the Castle of the Black Giant, Kai claimed to be a skilled sword-burnisher and Bedwyr a clever sharpener. In this way they and others of their company were allowed inside the castle. Once inside the walls Kai and Bedwyr boasted of their skills and bet the giant that they could cut off his head with one of their swords. The giant did not believe them and confidently thrust out his neck. In an instant Kai cut off his head. His companions sacked the castle and bore off the Black Giant's sword and all his treasure and took it to Arthur's court.

The next task was to find Mabon, son of Modron. First they had to free Mabon's kinsman, Eidol, from the prison in which his enemy Glivi was holding him.

At the request of Arthur Glivi released him at once. Eidol told them that to find Mabon they would have to ask the birds and the beasts and even the fishes. Some of the champions scorned such an idea, but Arthur urged them to do as they were advised. Alone among the companions Gwrhyr knew all human tongues and the languages of all creatures. He went first to the Ousel of Cilgwri, who said,

'When I first came here there was a smith's anvil, untouched except for the pecking of my beak every morning, and now the anvil is worn down to the size of a nut. Never in all my time have I heard of Mabon. But older than me is the Stag of Redynfre.'

So Gwyhyr enquired of that beast, who said,

'When I first came here there was a plain all

30

around me without any tree save an oak sapling which grew to be an oak of a hundred branches. Now nothing remains of that tree but a withered stump. Never in all my time have I heard of Mabon. But older than me is the Owl of Cwm Cowlyd.'

So Gwrhyr enquired of that bird, who said,

'When I first came here, this place was a wooded glen. And a race of men came and rooted up the trees. And there grew a second wood which was likewise cut down, and this wood you see is the third in this valley. My wings are withered stumps, and in all my time I have never heard of the man you seek. But older than me is the Eagle of Gwern Abwy.'

So Gwrhyr and his companions travelled on and enquired of that creature.

'When I first came here, I could peck at the stars from the summit of a high rock. Now that rock is but a

span high. And in all my time I have not heard of Mabon. But older than me is the Salmon of Llyn Llyw. When I came here I struck my talons into the Salmon, but he drew me down into the deep, and I scarcely escaped with my life. I sent my kindred to attack the fish, but at last he made peace with me, and besought me to take fifty fish-spears out of his back. Unless he knows something of the one you seek, I cannot tell you who may. I will guide you to him.'

So they went on, and the Eagle explained to the Salmon that these were Arthur's men on a quest, and that they sought news of Mabon the son of Modron. The Salmon replied,

'As much as I know I will say. With every tide I swim up the Severn river until I come near the walls of Gloucester, and there I have found such wrong as I never found elsewhere. Let two of you go with me riding me on each of my shoulders.'

Kai and Gwrhyr rode on the shoulders of the great Salmon until they could hear the wailing from inside the walls of the city. And it was the lamentation of Mabon whom they sought, and who could not be released for gold or silver or for any gifts of wealth, but only through battle. Then the companions returned to Arthur to beg his help and he summoned all his warriors to that place, and stormed the castle. Meanwhile Kai and Bedwyr went up the river once more on the shoulders of the Salmon, broke into the dungeon, and set the prisoner free.

But even though this task was accomplished, there yet remained four more. The next was to find the nine bushels of flax-seed which Yspaddaden had required of Kilhwch, to grow the flax for Olwen's bridal veil. Gwrhyr, who understood the language of ants, heard some of these creatures lamenting that a fire was threatening their habitation, whereupon he drew his sword and smote off the ant-hill, and carried it to safety on the blade of his great sword, and so it escaped being burnt in the fire. In gratitude the hoard of tiny ants rewarded Gwrhyr by gathering the nine bushels of flax-seed, in full measure without lacking any, except one flax-seed. And this last a lame ant brought in before nightfall.

Meanwhile Kai and Bedwyr went up to the top of the Five Peaks, which is Pumlumun, and there they saw a great plume of smoke afar off, which did not drift in the wind. And this was a sign to them that it was the fire of a robber. And indeed it was Dillus the Bearded who had made it, the greatest robber that ever fled from Arthur. Kai and Bedwyr observed the robber while he roasted

the flesh of a wild boar in the fire. Then, while he was gorging himself on the succulent meat, they set a trap for him. They dug a pit behind him, then, coming round in front of him, they struck him so that he fell backwards into it. Then they plucked out his beard which was to be woven into the leash that alone could hold the dogs needed for hunting the Great Riving Boar.

But first they had to go to North Britain to bring to bay the boar Ysgithrwyn, whose tusk alone could shave the beard of Yspaddaden. The hunting of this beast was dire, but it was nothing compared with the hunting of Twrch Trwyth, the Great Riving Boar of the Other Realms.

With the dogs, Aned and Aethlem, the companions set out in search of Twrch Trwyth. This boar had already laid waste a third part of Ireland, and there were certain precious things between his ears, a comb and a pair of golden shears, for he had once been a king that God had transformed into a swine for his sins. Gwrhyr spoke to him in the speech of swine. One of the Great Boar's offspring replied for him. This was Silver-Bristle, whose hide shone in the woodlands, and he replied that these treasures would never be yielded up unless the Riving Boar was slain. Meanwhile Twrch Trwyth and all his brood would go into Arthur's country and wreak all the mischief that was in their power.

The Riving Boar landed at Porth Clais in Dyfed with all his offspring. Arthur and his host caught up with them on Preselau Top. With Arthur were some of the men who had distinguished themselves in North Britain in the hunting of Ysgithrwyn. But even so four of Arthur's champions were slain. And in a second encounter in the same place four more were killed, though this time Twrch Trwyth himself was wounded. And between that place and Aberteifi the boar killed three other men, and one of these was Arthur's chief builder. And at Aberteifi two other men fell to the riving tusks, and the hunt continued eastward as far as the river Llychwr,

with many huntsmen and many dogs killed. From the time that Twrch Trwyth came out of the sea from Ireland, Arthur never had sight of him till then, and it was there, too, that many of the lesser swine were killed, so that only two of them were left alive. Still the Riving Boar made a stand, even against Arthur himself, so that many more dogs and men fell to the terrible tusks.

The hunt now changed direction, as Twrch Trwyth made for the headwaters of the Tawe, and then back westward over the Tywi to Ceredigion, then once again struck over the mountains eastward to Ystrad Yw, and everywhere he went he left a trail of death. A king of France and a king of Brittany were among his victims, and some of Arthur's kinsmen too. But by now all the Boar's brood lay dead, scattered along the hillsides, all except the Great Boar himself. At last they came to the banks of the Severn river. Arthur summoned the warriors of Cornwall and of Devon, and determined to force the Riving Boar into the river. Mabon the son of Modron, who had been so long imprisoned at Gloucester, assembled a host who came upon Twrch Trwyth between the Severn and the Wye, forced him into the water, and seized the shears from behind his ears, but they could not win the comb. For Twrch Trwyth was swift and agile in the manner of all swine, and neither man nor horse could overtake him until he reached Cornwall. And all their trouble was mere play compared with the bloody battle they fought to obtain the comb. When this too had been wrenched from the beast's head, Twrch Trwyth plunged into the sea at Land's End, taking with him the two dogs, Aned and Aethlem, who had hunted him so long, to return with them to the Other Realm under the waves. And this was the hunting of the Great Riving Boar.

Then Arthur rested in Cornwall and enquired, 'Is there any of the tasks yet unfulfilled?'

'Still we must get the blood of the Black Witch necessary for the shaving of Yspaddaden,' the champions told him. This woman was the daughter of the White Witch and she dwelt in the Valley of Affliction on the borders of Hell. So Arthur set forth and came to that place. And there were with him Gwynn the son of Nudd and Gwyther son of Greidiawl. Two of their servants went in to fight the crone, for it is not seemly for great warriors to be seen contending with a hag. But she drove them out of her cave. Then two others went in and she did with them likewise. So then Arthur set them all four on his great horse Llamrei the Prancer, and with them burst into the cavern. He drew his dreaded dagger Carnwennan, struck at the Black Witch and clove her in twain, so that she fell in two parts. And Kaw of North Britain took the black blood and kept it for the shaving of Yspaddaden.

Then Kilhwch, together with as many as wished ill to Yspaddaden, who were numerous, took all these trophies to the giant's castle. They showed him Mabon the son of Modron, free at last. They displayed to him the sword of Gwrnach the Black Giant. They laid out for him the nine bushels of flax-seed for the weaving of Olwen's bridal veil. They brandished the beard of Dillus the Robber, plaited into a leash for the hounds that had hunted Twrch Trwyth. And Kaw of North Britain showed him the gleaming sharp tusk of Ysgithrwyn, and a bowl of the blood of the Black Witch.

And Kaw of North Britain shaved his beard, skin and flesh, clean from ear to ear.

'Art thou shaved, man?' asked Kilhwch.

'I am shaved,' answered the giant.

'Is thy daughter mine now?'

'She is thine,' said the giant. 'It is Arthur who has accomplished this for thee. By my free will thou shouldst never have had her, for losing her I lose my life.'

So they cut off his head and placed it on a stake in the citadel. And they took possession of his castle and of his treasure. And that night Olwen became Kilhwch's bride, and she continued to be his wife for as long as they lived.

And the hosts of Arthur departed, each man to his own country.

# THE BRIDE OF
# FLOWERS

There was once a handsome fair-haired young man. Even as a baby his mother had refused to acknowledge him, and had decreed that he could have no name, nor be given arms and armour, nor yet have any wife of human kind. Others of his kindred, the powerful magicians, Math and Mathonwy, and his uncle Gwydion, were moved to pity the child's lot. And, being skilled in enchantment, they contrived that his mother, the lady Arianrhod, should be caused to undo all her mischief.

In the guise of shoemakers they enticed the unkind woman to a fitting of richly worked shoes. A wren flew down as she tried the shoes; the boy snatched his shoemaker's awl and hurled it at the bird, hitting it between the sinew and the bone, and that so squarely that Arianrhod cried out,

'With a steady hand did the lion aim at it!' Whereupon the magicians resumed their proper shapes, and told her that she had named her son Llew Llaw Gyffes, the Lion of the Steady Hand. And henceforth by that name was he known.

And again they deceived her by conjuring up the likenesses of armed warriors about to attack her castle by land and sea. Arianrhod hurriedly ordered the defenders of her fortress to muster for battle, and she herself, not knowing him in the throng of young men, gave arms and armour to the lad who by now was of an age to bear arms. All the noise of warlike tumult ceased forthwith. Again the magicians showed themselves in their true semblances, and told the lady that she had bestowed arms and armour on her son.

There remained now only to find a wife for the young man, which was a harder task than either of the other two, for if the maiden was of any race that

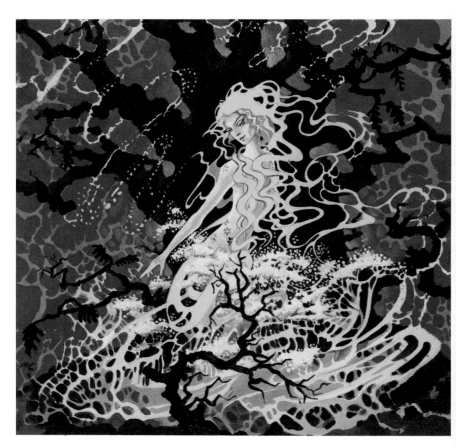

inhabited the earth, surely Arianrhod would know and would work her evil. So they took counsel, and by charms and illusions fashioned a bride of flowers. They took the blossom of the oak, and of the broom and of the meadowsweet, and produced from them the fairest and most graceful maiden that man ever saw. And they baptised her, and gave her the name of Blodeuwedd, which means the likeness of a flower.

The unkind lady Arianrhod, however, bitter at her defeat by those who wished Llew well, soon died.

Blodeuwedd became Llew's wife, and they lived happily in a castle in the confines of Ardudwy, where it borders on Eifionydd.

One day, while Llew was on a visit to Math and Mathonwy, and Blodeuwedd was walking in her garden, she heard the sound of a hunting-horn. Gronw Pebyr, the lord of Penllyn, was pursuing a stag, and when the chase was done, Blodeuwedd invited him to the castle. He accepted gladly, and he and his retinue dined and rested. From the moment that Blodeuwedd looked upon Gronw she became filled with love for him, and as he gazed upon her, the same feeling came to him. All their discourse was concerning the love and affection they felt for one another. When the time came for the huntsmen to leave, Blodeuwedd implored Gronw to stay longer. He stayed, and they spent their time discussing how they could bring about the death of Llew. Blodeuwedd knew that her husband was under powerful protection from his kindred, the magicians who had made her, and that he could only be slain by certain secret means. Therefore she resolved so to beguile Llew that he would disclose to her the manner in which he could be slain.

41

Gronw took his leave of Blodeuwedd, and Llew returned, all unsuspecting, to his castle. By her wiles and enticements the lady soon learned her husband's secret and the strange means by which alone he could be killed.

'Not easily can I be slain,' he said, 'except by a wound. And the spear wherewith I am struck must be a year in the forging. And no work must be done on it except during the Sacrifice on Sundays. Neither can I be slain in a house, nor outside a house, nor on horseback nor on foot, but by making a bathing place for me by the side of the river, and by putting a roof over the cauldron, and thatching it well and tightly, and by bringing a he-goat, and putting it beside the cauldron. Then, if I place my foot on the beast's back, and the other on the edge of the cauldron, whoever strikes me thus will cause my death.'

'Well,' she said, 'I thank Heaven that it will be easy to avoid this.'

No sooner had she learned Llew's secret than she sent to Gronw Pebyr. Gronw toiled at making the spear, and that day twelvemonth it was finished. He sent word to Blodeuwedd that he was ready to do what had to be done.

Then Blodeuwedd caused all the goats in the region to be gathered, and had them brought to the other side of the river from the bath-house which, unknown to Llew, she had specially made. The next day she spoke to Llew, and told him that a bath-house had been prepared, and urged him to go to the river with her to see it. Finding there the herd of goats, Blodeuwedd feigned surprise, but jokingly urged her husband to demonstrate to her the precise circumstances in which he could be slain.

He went willingly to the bath-house, placed one foot on the edge of the cauldron and the other on a goat's back. Thereupon Gronw, who had concealed himself nearby, rose up from the hill, rested on one knee, and flung the poisoned spear with unerring aim. It struck Llew full in the chest and he gave a fearful scream and flew up in the form of an eagle. And thenceforth he was no longer seen.

Gronw and Blodeuwedd went together into the palace that night, and Gronw took Blodeuwedd and all the possessions of Llew, together with his domain, so that both Ardudwy and Penllyn were under his sway.

Hearing of the cruel fate of Llew, Math and Mathonwy and Gwydion sought everywhere for him, until they heard of a certain vassal's sow, which always wandered to the same spot in the forest. They followed the sow the next time she was let out of her sty to forage for acorns and other swine-food, and she led them to a tree, where they saw an eagle in a pitiful condition. But despite this it seemed to Gwydion that the eagle was Llew. He sang verses to the bird, and coaxed it down until it perched on the lowest branch, and at last upon Gwydion's knee. Then Gwydion struck it with his magic wand, its feathers melted away and there stood Llew, returned to his own form. No-one ever saw a more piteous sight, for he was all skin and bone. They brought the best physicians in Gwynedd, and before the end of the year, he was quite healed.

'Lord,' he said to Math, 'I will have retribution.' So they called together all the host of Gwynedd, and set forth for the castle of Gronw and Blodeuwedd. Gronw withdrew further westward to the extremity of the land, and there Llew had his revenge on him in the manner of a warrior.

But Blodeuwedd fled in panic she knew not whither. Her handmaidens also fled with her, and in their confusion at the approach of the host of Gwynedd,

they were all drowned in the deep lake, which is Llyn y Morynion, the Lake of the Maidens.

Gwydion overtook Blodeuwedd and said to her, 'I will not slay thee, for I would do worse unto thee than that. I will turn thee into a bird; and because of the shame thou has brought upon Llew Llaw Gyffes, thou shalt never show thy face in the light of day henceforth; and that through fear of all the other birds. For it shall be their nature to attack thee, and to chase thee wheresoever they may find thee. And thou shalt not lose thy name, but always be called Blodeuwedd.'

So saying, he struck her with his magic wand. Her lovely features were changed, her beautiful big eyes became even larger, and shone balefully, her sweet mouth shrivelled and hardened into a vicious beak, her smooth cheeks sprouted thick feathers, her slim white form shortened and thickened, her delicate dainty feet became hard powerful claws. With a mournful hooting cry, she flew off to become a creature of the night and darkness, whose eerie call through the dark shadows can, to this day, chill the blood.

# THE LAND BENEATH THE WAVES

It is said that where the river Dyfi runs into Cardigan Bay the bells of vanished churches ring sadly under the water, tolled by the restless tides. And they toll for the lost Lowland Region, Cantref y Gwaelod, once a place of fertile fields, tall corn and prosperous towns nourished by plentiful harvests. Prince Gwyddno ruled over this land from his castle at the mouth of the Mawddach, and safeguarded it from the sea with a series of dykes and sluices which regulated the ebb and flow of the tides along that stormy coastline. These sea-works were solidly built, and Gwyddno took care that they should be well maintained. They were patrolled night and day, so that inside their protection, Gwyddno and all his sub-

jects could feel completely secure and free to enjoy the good life afforded by the fertility of their fields and their own industry and vigilance.

The keeper of the great dyke and all its works was Seithenyn, a prince of Dyfed. For many years he conscientiously attended to the duties of his office, for next to Gwyddno he held the highest honour in the land. But, like his lord, he enjoyed the pleasures that such a prosperous region so easily provided. No opportunity for a banquet or a carouse was ever missed in the Lowland Region. Feasting and drinking went on continuously. Indeed the Prince himself and his chief officer, the warden of the dyke, gave the lead and set the pace. In time what had begun gradually as an indulgence that could well be afforded developed into a dangerous addiction – the pursuit of pleasure for its own sake, regardless of all restraint. Life in the Lowland Region became a byword for extravagance and riotous living.

With all discipline relaxed the safeguards were neglected and the watches not properly kept. The great dyke began to suffer; the stonework was sapped and mined, the piles rotten and dislocated, the floodgates began to leak and fall apart. Gwyddno and Seithenyn and the specially picked corps of guardians seemed to be deaf to the danger and blind to the evidence of decay. Only the faithful Teithryn protested. The northern section of the dyke was under his control, and he was strict in the execution of his duty. He demanded an urgent meeting with Gwyddno and Seithenyn, but to no avail. He was detained for yet another banquet, and was beguiled by the beautiful daughter of Seithenyn, who always played a leading part in the merrymaking.

It was a dangerous season, the full moon of March, the moon of madness, of high spring tides and strong gales. As the sound of revelry grew louder Teithryn kept his wits about him, drinking little of the wine and mead that were put before him. He could see that Seithenyn and the others, incapable even of standing on their feet, were far beyond responding to any danger that might arise. So that when the moment came, as he knew it must, that the wild waves reached the feeble dyke, he quietly left the scene of the debauch and made his way to safety.

The great storm overwhelmed the dyke along the whole of its length, the raging tide swirled in over the Lowland Region, over its fields and farms and fine flourishing towns. Everything was swept away, every mortal being was drowned, except for a fortunate few who scrambled to a higher ground before Cantref y Gwaelod vanished for ever from human sight.

Seithenyn was among the first to perish, vainly trying to stem the waves by drawing his sword and rushing into the flood. His beautiful daughter had danced her last dance on dry land. She and all her fine ladies moved now to the swaying of the waves.

49

Gwyddno, once lord of the richest of lands, was glad to reach the firm ground of Ardudwy, where he knew that he and the few followers who escaped with him could only sustain themselves henceforward by laborious toil in a harsh land.

The sea towards Ireland was grown wider than it had been in former times, but still at the lowest of tides the vengeful waters will relent and allow glimpses of drowned forests, remains of dykes, and the pathetic foundations of what were once proud buildings.

# THE DREAM OF MAXEN WLEDIG

Maxen Wledig was Emperor of Rome, and one day when he was out hunting with thirty-two kings who were his vassals, he rested from the chase and slept awhile in the heat of the day. And he dreamed that he journeyed over many lands until he came to what seemed to him to be the fairest island in the whole world, with a mountain as high as the sky, and at the foot of it a great city and a vast castle of many towers. The castle gates were open, so he went into the great hall, and there he saw two comely young men playing at chess with golden pieces on a silver board, and a powerful old man on a chair of ivory, and before him a maiden seated on a chair of gold and she was the fairest sight that ever man beheld.

In his dream he threw his arms about her neck and sat by her on her chair, and the chair was not less roomy for both of them than for the maiden alone. But the dream did not last. The restlessness of the hounds and the neighing and prancing of horses aroused the Emperor from his sweet sleep. For a week he could do

little but think of the maiden. He called his wisest
counsellors and told them of his dream. They advised
him to have the whole world searched for three years.
But the search was in vain. Then the King of the Romans
suggested to the Emperor that he should go hunting
again in the place where he had the dream, on the banks
of a river flowing westwards.

So the Emperor returned to the place and
dreamed again of the castle, and of the comely young
men, of the powerful old man seated on a chair of ivory
and of the beautiful maiden seated on a chair of gold.
And when he awoke he recounted all his dream to his
messengers and thirteen of them went out, each with a
sign of peace, and eventually they came to a place they
recognized as the land their master had described to
them, and the land was the Island of Britain.

They crossed the island until they came to Snow-
don, and saw Anglesey and Arfon all before them, and
the castle at the mouth of the river and all as the
Emperor had seen in his dream: the open portal, the two
young men playing at chess, the old man on the ivory
chair, and best of all the lovely lady on the chair of gold.
The messengers knelt before her and hailed her as
Empress of Rome. At first she was unwilling to believe
their words were anything but mockery. But eventually
she said,

'If the Emperor loves me, let him come here and
seek me.'

And so the messengers returned to Rome to tell the Emperor that they had seen the woman he loved, and knew her name and her kindred and her race. She was the lady Helen, daughter of Eudav and sister to Kynan and Adeon.

The Emperor immediately set forth with his army and the messengers were his guide. When they came to Britain they were attacked by Beli, the son of Manogan and his sons, but they drove them into the sea. Then they went forward to Arfon, and everything was as he had seen in his dream, with Kynan and Adeon playing at chess, Eudav on his ivory chair and Helen on the chair of gold.

'Empress of Rome,' he said, 'all hail,' and threw his arms about her neck.

That night she became his bride. The lady Helen's dowry from her father was the Island of Britain, from the Narrow Sea to the sea towards Ireland, together with the three isles adjacent, which are Man, Wight and Anglesey. And three castles were to be made for her wherever she desired. The chief of these was to be at Caernarfon. There they brought earth from Rome that it might be more healthful for the Emperor. After that two castles were made, one at Carmarthen and another at Caerleon.

Helen also caused roads to be built throughout the island, that are called to this day Sarn Helen, meaning the Roads of Helen of the Legions.

Seven years the Emperor remained with Helen. But the Roman custom forbad such a long absence, so they made a new Emperor.

When Maxen heard this, he set forth towards Rome. On the way he vanquished every enemy in his path, but the city of Rome itself was well fortified. For a whole year Maxen and his army laid siege to it and encamped before it. After a year there came the brothers of Helen, Kynan and Adeon, and a small host with them, and attacked the city more expertly than those already engaged in the siege. They scaled the walls with ladders which they had specially made, stormed the city and sacked it. The false Emperor fell, and many others with him. The gates of Rome were opened and Maxen sat upon his throne, and said to Kynan and Aedon,

'I now have possession of the whole of my empire. This host I give unto you, to vanquish whatever region you may desire in the whole world.'

# RHONABWY'S DREAM

Rhonabwy and two companions were on a quest through the plains of Powys when they came upon an old black hall with a smoky fire tended by a crone. The people of the hall were surly, but gave the travellers a meagre supper of barley bread, cheese, and milk and water. The floor was dirty and the couches were mere straw covered with old rags and threadbare sheets. But there was also a yellow calfskin stretched out, and it was a privilege to sleep on it. And there Rhonabwy slept.

And this was the strange dream that came to him. It seemed to him that he and his companions were journeying towards the River Severn. A fierce rider on a chestnut horse overtook them, and told them that he had been one of the messengers between Arthur and his nephew Medrawd, and it was he who had kindled the strife between them that led to the battle of Camlann, where both were slain. Three nights before the battle, this man, Iddawc, had fled to North Britain, to do penance for seven years.

In the dream another rider whom Iddawc told them was Rhuvawn, the son of Prince Deorthach, overtook them on a bay horse, and they came to the ford of

Rhyd y Groes over the Severn, where there was a great encampment. Arthur himself was there, on an island below the ford, together with many tall knights.

'Where, Iddawc, didst thou find these little men?' asked Arthur.

'Upon the road,' said Iddawc.

Arthur laughed, and said,

'It grieves me that men of such stature as these should have this island in their keeping, after the men that guarded it of yore.'

Then Iddawc told Rhonabwy to look at the stone in the ring on Arthur's finger.

'It is one of the properties of that stone to enable thee to remember what thou hast seen here tonight. Hadst thou not seen that stone thou wouldst never have remembered anything.'

Then Rhuvawn and his troop came up, and they and all their horses were of one colour, as red as blood. Yet another troop came to the ford, and their mounts were whiter than the lily from their chests upward, and

blacker than jet below. They were the host of Adaon the son of Taliesin.

But now it was time for them all to go with Arthur to the battle of Badon. There came with them a troop in pure white riding jet-black horses; these were the men of Norway. And yet another troop rode with them of the men of Denmark, all clad in black and mounted on white horses.

And all the hosts rode off together. Iddawc and Rhonabwy dismounted, and soon they heard the noise of a great battle. They saw Kai, Arthur's best horseman, and Kador, Earl of Cornwall, with the sword of Arthur that bore the likeness of two gold serpents. And when the sword was drawn from the scabbard it seemed as if two flames of fire burst from the jaws of the serpents.

And in his dream Rhonabwy saw Arthur seated on a great golden chair playing a game of chess with the chieftain Owain, the son of Urien, with gold pieces on a board of silver. But a messenger ran in and told Owain that Arthur's pages and attendants were harrassing and tormenting his ravens.

'Play thy game,' said Arthur.

And a second messenger came with the same story, and again Arthur said,

'Play thy game,' to Owain.

But when a third messenger came, Owain told him,

'Go back and wherever thou findest the strife at the thickest, there lift up thy banner, and let come what pleases Heaven.'

And, with the suddenness of a dream, all the ravens rose in the air, swept down on their tormentors and wrought great havoc on them. Another messenger came and reported to Arthur that the ravens of Owain were slaying his young men.

'Forbid thy ravens,' said Arthur to Owain.

'Play thy game,' said Owain.

And so it went on until yet another knight rode up on a piebald horse, imploring Arthur to bring an end to the battle. Arthur took the golden chessmen that were on the board and crushed them till they became as dust, and besought Owain to forbid his ravens. Owain ordered his banner to be lowered and all was peace.

And when Rhonabwy awoke he was on the yellow calfskin, having slept there three nights and three days. And the dreams he dreamt there troubled him to the end of his days.

# SAINT DAVID

You may have heard it said that a Welshman can do anything except stand six feet tall. Whether this is true or not, the greatest of the Saints of God in Wales was a man of small stature, though in every other respect he stands among the most impressive figures in our history.

In his day the old tales of marvel were well-remembered, dreams and omens still held sway in men's minds. Signs and wonders attached themselves as easily to the new Christian faith as they had to the beliefs of the older world. Almost as soon as it was preached in Palestine the Good News reached our shores, brought along the roads of Rome by soldiers and traders of a great empire.

But like all empires of this world the days of Rome were numbered. When David was born, the legions had long marched home, and the civilization they had brought to Britain was under attack from barbarian invaders. The unsubdued Irish descended upon the western coasts, captured as many Britons as they could and sold them into slavery. The Saxons prowled the Narrow Sea and set up their pirate kingdoms in East

Britain. Maxen Wledig had taken all the best fighting men back with him to Rome in his bid for imperial power.

In a darkening world only a few cherished the flame of faith. One of the Britons sold into slavery was Patrick, who was to convert his captors from their old ways. An angel appeared to him in dreams on a headland in Dyfed at the meeting of three roads, where he and a few followers sought to establish a place for prayer. He learned that he was to leave that place to another who was to come after him. At first Patrick was angry, but the angel made him look westward across the sea, and there he saw the whole land of the Irish spread out before him, and he understood that his mission was to be among that people, and he embarked immediately on his life's work in that country.

In due course David came to the place where Patrick had seen the angel. David was the son of the King of Ceredigion, and close kin, it was said, to Arthur himself. He was brought for baptism to Bishop Elvis, who was blind. There a spring of water appeared where none had been seen before. After the baptism the holy man sprinkled his own face with the water from the spring, and his sight was restored.

The boy dwelt in a valley on that headland and dedicated himself to a life of learning, reading, prayer and fasting and good works. He became the head of a little community of brethren. The valley grew fertile and fruitful from the labour of their hands, for their life was one of service not only to the Lord but to their native

64

land as well. Many of the brethren went out and founded other such communities, and as David's fame increased so the tales that were told about him multiplied also.

The brethren were occupied not only with the disciplines necessary for deepening knowledge and understanding of the scriptures, they were also obliged to work hard to maintain the monastery by all the diligence of good husbandry, and by the practice of all the many crafts needful for survival. One of the brethren was an adept keeper of bees. Such was the affection of these little creatures for their keeper that, when he was sent on a mission across the sea to Ireland, the bees followed him and clustered on the prow of his ship. He had the ship turned back and the bees went to their hives. Then he set out again, and again the same thing happened. When it happened a third time, David blessed the bees and sent them to Ireland, and there they flourished, although until that time no bees had ever been known to thrive there. Equally, from that sending forth from Dyfed, no bees ever flourished in David's monastery.

Although they were sorely beset by their many enemies, the Britons were not free from dissension among themselves, and it became necessary to call together a great gathering where the points at issue could be discussed and settled. The appointed place was on the banks of the Brefi in Ceredigion, on an open meadow, where a large crowd assembled. It was such a noisy and quarrelsome gathering that the presiding bishops could not make themselves heard, and the ground was so level that they could hardly be seen. But

David placed a handkerchief on the ground and stood upon it. At once the ground rose up in a hill. From this eminence David preached to the people. He spoke so eloquently that all dissension was stilled. His voice was heard from afar, and it is said that a white dove flew down and rested upon his shoulder. To this day the hill at Llanddewi Brefi is pointed out as the scene of one of David's most memorable sermons.

As David's life drew to its close, the signs and wonders multiplied. The voices of angels were heard, the church filled with heavenly music and sweet fragrance. Knowing that his end was near, he spoke to the brethren,

'Guard your faith, be steadfast in your conduct, and be mindful of the little things.'

The voice that had rung out from the hill of Brefi was still at last on earth, but in the minds of his fellow-countrymen it has never been silent, and it was to guide and inspire them in all the many struggles that were to lie ahead of them in the next fifteen hundred years.

# GELERT

Never was there finer hunting in the mountains, nor handsomer horses and hounds than when Prince Llewelyn rode out to the chase. And of all his pack the most famous was Gelert, the massive wolfhound that had been given to him by the King of England as part of the dowry when he had married the king's daughter. Welsh hounds are well adapted to the difficult country they hunt in. They can keep going all day and they give tongue musically so that the quarry can always be found. But among all the pack Gelert was special. He was much taller than the others and was kept for the most important duties. A fit companion, everyone said, for a Prince.

When the hunt was summoned to the meet, Gelert did not go with the others, but stood guard over the cradle of Llewelyn's young son in the hunting-lodge in the forest, where all the court were assembled for a good day in the open air. The child and the huge dog were firm friends, and it was no hardship for Gelert to stay indoors for once and frolic with the little boy.

In the evening the hunting party returned, tired out and well satisfied with their day's work. But what was this? No greeting from Gelert, who usually bounded to meet the Prince on his return. Llewelyn approached the silent chambers. He opened the door and a scene of horror met his eyes. Blood was spattered everywhere and the room was in chaos. In the middle of it all stood Gelert – with blood on his muzzle!

Llewelyn could hardly believe that his favourite hound had killed his son, but why else should the dog be covered in blood? Llewelyn drew his sword and, heedless of the dog's reproachful eyes, thrust the blade deep into Gelert's body.

At that very moment a weak cry came from under the tumbled coverlets of the overturned cradle. Still wild with anger and sorrow, the Prince threw aside the bloodstained bedclothes, and there was his son, safe and sound and smiling up at him. And there, too, an enormous wolf lay dead, its throat torn out by the loyal Gelert.

There had clearly been a fierce struggle before the beast met its end, and Llewelyn had fatally misunderstood the signs. But by now those imploring eyes had closed in their last sleep. They were to haunt Llewelyn for a long time. He had the body honourably buried, and Gelert's grave, Bedd Gelert, can still be seen. The Prince became a wise and just ruler, never again acting in the heat of the moment. He enjoyed a long reign, and is honoured by his people as Llewelyn the Great. But to the end of his life he could never forget the sad eyes of the faithful Gelert.

# THE LADY OF
# THE LAKE

In the valley of Myddfai in the heart of the Black
Mountains lived Rhiwallon. He lived alone with his
widowed mother and tended the few cattle which provided them their meagre livelihood. Early one morning,
on his way to the little lake of Llyn y Fan that lies in the
shadow of the highest peak, he saw a lovely lady sitting
on the smooth surface of the water and combing her long
golden hair. He fell in love with her at once, but all he
had to offer her at the time was some barley bread from
his herdsman's pouch. She refused his offer, eluded his
grasp and dived under the water, saying,

'*Cras dy fara, Nid hawdd fy nala.*' Hard is thy bread,
hard am I to hold.

Rhiwallon determined to make another effort to
woo the beautiful lady, and on the advice of his mother
went up again next morning with some soft, unbaked
dough. Again the lady appeared, and again she refused
what he had to offer, saying,

'*Llaith dy fara, Ti ni fynna.*' Soft is thy bread, thee I
will not have.

Still Rhiwallon persisted, for by now his heart was entirely set on winning the hand of the lady of the lake. Again he sought the advice of his mother. This time she baked barley bread for him which was neither too hard nor too soft, and with this offering he succeeded in his heart's desire. But his happiness was short-lived, for there now appeared from under the surface of the water a noble old man of great stature, accompanied by another maiden who could have been the twin sister of the lady of the lake.

'I give my consent to your marriage with one of my daughters,' said the old man, 'but first you must satisfy me that you can distinguish which of them is the true object of your affections.'

This was no easy task, for the two girls were perfect counterparts of one another, and however narrowly Rhiwallon scanned the two he failed to perceive the least difference between them.

But one of the girls lowered her gaze and moved her foot slightly forward. Rhiwallon immediately noticed that there was a slight difference in the lacing of her sandals, and from that he knew his true love. The venerable father immediately gave his consent to the match, and called up the bride's dowry from under the lake, such cattle as had never been seen in the valley. But it was the bride herself who laid down a condition that did not seem onerous to the young man, that she would stay with him until she received from him three blows without cause.

And so they lived happily for some years and had three fine sons. One day there was a christening in the neighbourhood, to which everyone was invited. Rhiwal-

lon noticed that his wife showed some reluctance on the
way to the church, and she made the excuse that she had
left her gloves at home. Her husband ran back to fetch
them and when he caught up with her he tapped her
lightly on the shoulder with one of them. And that was
the first blow without cause.

Some time later they were invited to a wedding,
and to Rhiwallon's discomfiture his wife burst into tears
in the middle of the celebrations. He touched her lightly
in reproof. She said,

'I am weeping because I forsee the sorrows that
lie ahead for this young couple.'

And that was the second blow without cause.

The years passed and Rhiwallon was very careful not to do anything that would cause their happiness and prosperity to be impaired. Then one of their neighbours died, and the couple had to attend the funeral. Once again Rhiwallon was bewildered by his wife's behaviour, for she seemed to be in the best of spirits, laughing loudly. She said that she laughed because the dead have no troubles, and when again he lightly touched her in reproof, that was accounted the third blow without cause.

Immediately she left the gathering and went back to the farm, calling all the cattle by their names and the other stock as well. And they all followed the lady to the lake, and with her walked into its waters and disappeared from sight for ever. The four oxen that were pulling the plough went with them, taking the plough also and leaving the marks of the furrow that may still be seen leading into the lake. Even a little black calf that had recently been slaughtered wriggled off the hook in the kitchen where it had been hanging and joined all the other animals that were now called home by the lady of the lake.

But that is not the end of the story. For the three sons of Rhiwallon were by now growing into handsome young men of great ability and learning. From time to time the lady appeared to them, and taught them many things about the plants and herbs and berries of the mountains, their medicinal qualities and their virtues. She told the young men that they were to become benefactors to mankind, and furnished them with pre-scriptions and instructions for the preservation of health. The young men did not neglect her teachings and they became in the fullness of time the famous Physicians of Myddfai, *Meddygon Myddfai*, and they and their descen-dants for many generations afterwards ministered to the health of the people, and were honoured by princes.

# THE CURSE OF PANTANNAS

In the woodlands of the Taff valley, in the fields of Pantannas, there was a noisy and boisterous tribe – the Little People.

A husbandman called Rhydderch was so determined to be rid of these tiresome people that he consulted a witch. She agreed to help him if he gave her one evening's milking on his farm and one morning's. Her advice was to plough up all the places where the revels were held, for if the Little People found their green sward gone they would take offence and never return to trouble him. Rhydderch followed this advice and the singing and laughter that had so long tormented him was no longer heard, while his newly-ploughed fields flourished fruitfully with good crops of grain. But just as the harvest was to be carried to the barn, one of the Little People appeared, clad in the red jacket of his kind. Pointing an accusing finger at the husbandman, he called loudly,

'Vengeance cometh. Fast it approacheth.'

That night a great noise was heard, the house shook and a loud voice outside repeated,

'Vengeance cometh.' And so it was. For all the fields burnt in the night as if by fire, and not a grain of the harvest could be reaped, nor even any straw. And the red-jacketed figure again appeared to Rhydderch and called out,

'It but beginneth.'

Whereupon the husbandman promised that he would let his fields lie fallow once again, so that the revels of the Little People could continue as in the past. In return the little man promised that no further calamity should fall upon him nor upon his children.

And so it fell out. The farm prospered and the family also, until the third generation. Then an alliance was proposed between Rhydderch's grandson and the

daughter of a neighbouring farm. The misfortune that had befallen the grandfather was now but a faint memory, and all the neighbourhood was looking forward to the wedding feast at Pantannas. As the guests gathered, a loud voice was heard outside the house, crying,

'The time for vengeance has come.'

And, as in time past the building shook as if in a great storm. The young bridegroom rushed out into the night to find out the cause of the tumult, while the rest of the company waited for him indoors. They were to wait a very long time, for he was never seen again. And that night revelry of the Little People ceased also. When the family enquired of an old hermit who lived nearby, he explained to them (for he remembered the times of Rhydderch) that the judgment on Pantannas had now been fulfilled, and there was no possibility that any living

person would ever set eyes on the missing man. And what had happened to him?

He had run out into the darkness and there had met the Little People, who welcomed him and invited him to join in their merrymaking. Forgetful of his own wedding feast, he stayed with them for a few days. Then, deciding it was high time to go back home, he took his leave of his kind hosts. They led him to a spot which he recognized as being not far from his family's farm. But when he entered the house everything was changed. No-one recognized him, and some of the people said he was mad when he told them who he was.

'There was a man of your name once,' said one of them. 'My grandfather told me an old tale about him, the heir of Pantannas who disappeared on his wedding eve. But that,' he said, 'was hundreds of years ago.'

# THE HAUNTING
# OF THE RED
# CASTLE

Long ago people of quality used to set aside a corner of their fields for growing flax. It was the custom for travelling spinsters to spin the flax into linen yarn, and many a poor woman earned her living in this way. One such woman came one evening to the Red Castle of the March, where the Lords of Powys lived. The lord's steward welcomed the woman because he knew of old that she was a diligent spinner, and he set her to work at the wheel. There was more work for her on the morrow, so, according to custom, she was offered meat and drink and a lodging for the night.

Three of the servants, each with a candle in her hand, led the spinster to the room where she was to sleep, and she marvelled that such a grand room should be made ready for a mere spinning woman such as herself.

It had a boarded floor and two sash windows, and in the corner there was an elegant bed spread with soft covers. The servants made up a good fire and placed for her a table and a chair before it, and a lighted candle on the table. Bewildered by this unaccustomed reception, she gazed about her for some time, marvelling at the panelled room and the fine furniture. But then she composed herself and turned to reading the Good Book which was always with her wherever she travelled. While she was reading she heard the room door open, and turning her head, she saw a gentleman enter in gold-laced hat and waistcoat and the rest of his dress equally rich. He walked across to the sash window in the corner of the room, and then to the other window, and stood by it in a pensive attitude.

From her frequent visits to the castle the woman was familiar with the appearance of all who lived there, from the lord himself down to the stable-lads. This gentleman was a complete stranger. And he looked as if he wanted to say something to her, and as if he expected her to say something to him. But she remained silent, and after a little time he walked off, closing the door behind him as the servants also had done.

The good woman concluded that this was an apparition, and that she had been put in that room on purpose. Immediately she addressed herself to her prayers. As she was praying the man came in again, but she was still too agitated to speak to him, and could not utter a word. Again he walked out of the room in silence. Again she prayed for strength, and determined that if he came back once more she would indeed speak to him if she possibly could.

When, as she expected, he returned, she questioned him,

'Pray sir, who are you, and what do you want?'

He said, 'Take up the candle and follow me, and I will tell you.'

Taking up the candle, the woman followed the man out of the room. He led her along a long boarded passage to another room that was not much more than a large closet. He opened the door and entered, saying to the woman as he did so,

'Walk in, I will not hurt you.' Then he said, 'Observe what I do.' And he stooped down and took up one of the floor boards. Under it was a box with an iron handle. Then he showed the woman a crevice in the wall where, he said, a key was hid that would open the box. 'This box and key must be taken out and sent to the Earl in London. Will you see it done?'

'I will do my best,' was the woman's reply.

'Do,' he said, 'and I will trouble this house no more.' Then he walked out of the room.

As soon as the ghost had gone the woman called out and the steward and his wife came in at once, and all the other servants with lighted candles, as if they had been waiting to see the outcome of the interview. She told them that the man was very civil, and had been careful to affright her as little as possible. She showed them the box, and the servants found the key, and carried both off immediately, and a very heavy box it seemed to be.

And that, for the time being, seemed to be the end of the story, for she did not see the box opened, or ever found out what it contained. But she was never to forget till the end of her days what was to happen next.

The people of the castle told the woman that the room had been disturbed for a long time, so that nobody could sleep peacefully in it. Knowing her to be a God-fearing woman who never went anywhere without the Good Book, they decided to lodge her in the haunted chamber, and see what came of it. The steward took the box to the Earl in London, as the apparition had instructed, and within only the briefest time, he returned. She still did not know who the apparition was, or what the box had contained. The secret was never to be revealed nor the identity of the gentleman in the rich, old-fashioned clothes ever to be disclosed, nor what tale of scandal or mystery lay behind the hauntings. But the steward returned with instructions from the Earl that the spinning-woman was to be invited to remain as part of the household of the castle for as long as she wished, and that for the rest of her days she should be comfortably provided for.

And from that time forward, the Red Castle of the March was not visited by any apparition.

# THE HAZEL STAFF

A drover called Huw had driven his herd of small black cattle to the great city of London, where he knew that their tender meat would command a good price. It was a journey that he and many of his fellows made every year, for it was a thriving trade. The Drovers' Roads were well-trodden, the lodgings and taverns on the way provided a special welcome for the men from the mountains of Wales. Every drover had his corgi dogs which chivied the cattle and kept them moving, while he rode ahead on his sturdy Welsh pony to make sure that the way was safe for the slow-moving beasts. To guide his charges he carried a stout staff, which also served as a cudgel when need be. Some of these staffs were carefully carved and skilfully decorated, and Huw was particularly proud of his.

When he had sold his cattle for a fair price, Huw set off again for the hills of Wales. As he was crossing London Bridge, a stranger stopped him and enquired where such a fine staff had been cut, and in what parish the tree had grown which had produced such a handsome piece of wood. Huw became suspicious immediately, for this was not his first journey away from home, and he knew enough about the ways of great cities to be slow and hesitant in his reply. For the tree had grown and the stick had been cut in his own parish in the mountains, a place abounding in strange stories and legends of ancient times. He told him nonetheless, for the stranger seemed to be too aged and venerable to be any sort of robber. And when the stranger explained that the tree grew in a spot where treasure lay hidden, Huw's suspicions diminished, and he was persuaded to name the place.

Huw invited the stranger to return with him, and within only a few days they were riding through the green hills of Glamorgan, for the homeward journey, without any cattle to tend, was always as swift as the outward journey was slow. Huw led the stranger to the very tree where he had cut the staff only a few weeks before, the bark still plainly showing the tell-tale marks of the axe. This was indeed the place the old man had expected. Huw dug at the roots of the tree, and soon uncovered a broad flat stone. Between them, with much exertion they lifted the stone, and under the stone there was the entrance to a cave. Cautiously they penetrated the darkness, and there, in the shadows, they saw a great bell. The old man warned Huw that he was on no account to touch the bell, for its slightest sound would bring misfortune.

They pressed on, and the cave opened out into a high hall full of warriors armed and accoutred in the fashion of ancient times. And all were asleep. And on his throne in their midst was Arthur, as recognizable to them by his crown and great sword as by the dignity of his person. But all slept. And all about were the heaps of gold and silver and precious stones that were the tribute won by Arthur and his men in their wars.

Huw's guide explained in a whisper that the treasure was there for the taking, but only so much as a man might carry in his pockets. Huw needed no second bidding, and soon his pockets were heavy with gold. He noticed the old man stood by without taking a single coin, saying,

'He that hath wisdom desireth no greater wealth.'

And as they prepared to leave the cave, the old man spoke again, to warn Huw that he must on no account touch the great bell,

'For,' he said, 'at its sound perchance a warrior will awake, and ask aloud, "Is it the day?" And the day they await is the redemption of Wales from all the perils that beset her. Answer thou then, "No, sleep on." And make what escape thou may.'

So cautioned, Huw went quietly with his companion until they came again to the great bell. The old man, unencumbered with gold, passed it by without any difficulty, but the pockets of the greedy drover were bulging with gold. In the narrow space, he brushed against the bell, which gave forth a low trembling sound.

Whereat one of the warriors stirred in his sleep, raised his head, and cried out,

'Is it the day?'

Remembering what he had been told, Huw quickly called out, 'No, sleep on.'

And the warrior sunk his head again in sleep. They pressed ahead, and soon the explorers were out of the cave, and stood alone in daylight.

In gratitude to his benefactor, Huw now tried to press upon him at least a handful of the gold he had taken from the cave, but, meeting with a refusal, he turned to the task of covering the entrance so that no wayfarer should stumble upon its secret. And when he raised his head again, the old man had gone.

Huw returned to his work of droving, but his way of life was less frugal than formerly, and his dealings less meticulous. And sooner than he ever thought possible, his treasure was all spent. He consoled himself, however, that he now knew where he could replenish his store, for the wealth in the cave under the hazel tree seemed inexhaustible.

For the second time Huw made his way to the place, identified the tree, dug up the huge stone, and opened the entrance to the cave. Again he entered its shadows, and made his cautious way around the bell. There they all still were, Arthur and his warriors, awaiting the call. And there, too, was the treasure of their conquests, shining in the dark. More greedily than on his first visit, Huw filled his pockets with gold, so full that he could hardly stand, or move forward with his load. But he remembered how quickly his first treasure had disappeared, so that he was determined to take as much as he could carry. Weighed down with the heavy gold, he crawled slowly and painfully through the cave until he came to the bell. Encumbered as he was, he fell heavily against it, so that it clanged aloud with a terrifying sound that seemed to fill the cavern and aroused the sleeping warriors, and even Arthur himself. And a great shout arose,

'Is it the day?'

In his confusion Huw blurted out he knew not what, anything but the one true word which would have returned the host to their repose. Whereupon they beat him sorely, and thrust him out of the cavern. Bruised and shaken, he found himself again on the hillside he knew so well, and when he searched in his pockets he found they were full of dead leaves.